COPPER POX POISONING
by Karcian Suragh

This book is a work of fiction based on real events that occurred over a period of time.

Any resemblance to persons, living or dead, or places, events or locales is purely coincidental. The characters were real at some point in time but are still a re-production of the author's imagination.

Adult Reading Material
ISBN Number: 9798841401773

blimekronwing73@gmail.com

Dedication

This book is dedicated in memory of Mr. and Mistress Ben whom I knew since my teenage days. I am thankful for the attention they gave me and the opportunity to be present in their situation, I have no regret in being part of Ben's journey, in many ways seeing these things helped shape my own life and beliefs.

Table of Contents

Introduction

"Our great grandparents once said the older you grow the wiser you become. It is said that wisdom belongs to the aged, and understanding to the old. (Job 12:12 KJV - With the ancient is wisdom, and in length of days, understanding.)

Copper Coin Poisoning
When I first came across this unusual subject it was more than four decades ago, during my early teens. I am writing from firsthand knowledge, this was no vision, neither a dream nor an invented idea of mine but my reality. It happened and I pondered on it ever since.

My next-door neighbor was terminally ill with copper pox poisoning, strange enough as a present witness then to Mr. Ben's pain and suffering, I remembered he offered the doctor the sum of ten thousand dollars in cash or any amount to get him better. The doctor refused, he told Ben that he was unable and couldn't help him.

He said, "only God can help you and you contracted this sickness from a woman."

Mr. Ben passed away a short-while-after, believe it or not these practices did exist in the past and can still happen today, through the correct procedures. Weird as this may sound, copper pox poisoning is a very real disease unknown to the world and it has no cure whatsoever.

The reason I write on this topic is to open people's eyes and expose this uncommon disease. Also to raise awareness because people have all rights to ask questions, to know and learn about each and every existing disease there is on earth, in doing so, we can protect ourselves and help prevent others from being infected."

Karcian Suragh, Author

Copper Coin Pox Disclaimer

I am not held liable, neither have any sound evidence to support the statements made hereafter. My research over the years became tiresome. There was absolutely no consistent finding for this claim and it has not been scientifically proven anywhere in the world, making it futile at times to get information. As I figured out this topic/matter I know my theory could be wrong and can be corrected in that context. However, I am going to explain, in the best way I know from real observations.

Generations of today have little knowledge and are not familiar with this topic, if they do then it was told by an elder. My father said when he was a boy in Grenada, he knew of copper pox poisoning to a certain extent, and today at the age of eighty-five, he says it's been around for hundreds of years but believes it could be of Caribbean origin.

Everyone has a difference of opinion regarding some clarification on the subject, throughout my interviews with persons about copper pox poisoning most of the answers were inconsistent, the oral technique was more popular, while intercourse was less known to others. Even though this approach was less effective and less harmful, for men especially.

These are some of the outbreaks affiliated with copper pox poisoning: Dry rash, small reddish boils against the skin, signs of weakness, tiredness and other unknown symptoms that may be associated with the disease.

<u>WARNING</u>

Please do not attempt this dangerous method as an experiment on yourself and others whether for revenge on a failing relationship, ending of a marriage or as an avenue for benefits. Using these types of practices are harmful and can result in fatality from consumption, it is said to be a self-inflicted disease that can only be transmitted from a woman to a man during sexual activities.

The Alledged Process

As a reminder I am no medical practitioner, but here are some theories on how it is done or is suspected to be executed through local rumor mills.

1. The woman can take a copper coin, of one or five cent and place in her mouth beneath the tongue unknowing to her partner before giving oral sex.

She does this as follows:

> Staying tight lipped until he discharges into her mouth. This course of action can be risky depending on the partner. If the man's technique is deep thrusting, with the constant impact she will encounter difficulties in breathing and the coin may displace down her windpipe.

2. Alternatively, she may suck on the copper coin and keep ingesting the liquid substance while having intercourse with her partner, until he orgasms, this can be done repeatedly.

3. The woman can suck on the copper coin to accumulate enough saliva in her mouth form-

ing a golden brownish liquid. She waits for the moment when he ejaculates inside of her and swallows the liquid, which is supposed to flow through the arteries of the blood stream into his penis, therefore it enters the groin area directly where it was targeted. This supposedly leaves the woman unharmed which cannot be a surety because it can be assumed that is also slow poisoning for her especially if it remains in her body without treatment such as a detox, flushing with simple purified water or a visit to the doctor.

Once the process is properly done as planned, the side effects will be felt by the man, for which there is no cure.

It is necessary that the woman be secretive, positioning herself away from direct face to face contact with her partner during sexual intercourse because of the need to hide the copper coin in her mouth. The positions suggested are 'doggie style', any position that avoids kissing during sex, also positions that avoid lying backward in bed to avoid suffocation from the coin and even death. These are noted to be telltale signs that something is wrong.

The penis before final erection, discharges pre-ejaculation fluids, and it is assumed that the penis inside the vagina is like a sponge in water that absorbs upon ejaculation which is why it is believed that this type of silent poisoning will work. Diseases can enter a man's penis from vagina fluids during intercourse, this can enter a man's body through the tip or foreskin of the penis when one has unprotected sex.

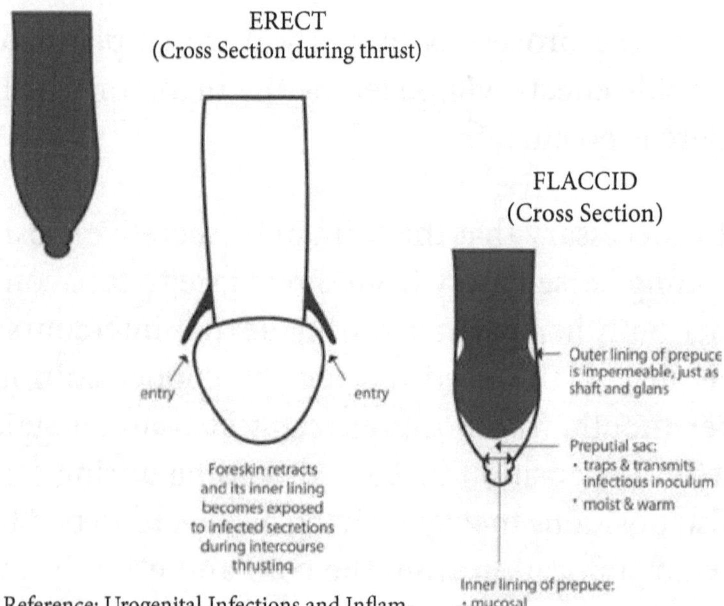

Reference: Urogenital Infections and Inflammations - https://books.publisso.de/en/publisso_gold/publishing/books/overview/52/81

My *Testimony*

"*I encountered this discovery many years ago between my neighbor who was a married man and his outside lover. Never a dull moment with them, until their relationship began deteriorating downhill. There was an incident where a doctor was caring for this man in the aftermath of diagnosis, administering two injections per day to ease his pain. The old Chinese physician stood together with me in the room watching Mr. Ben in pampers as he lay helpless on his bed weeping. At the time, being young and not really understanding everything I asked questions. 'So doc what seems to be the situation with Mr. Ben?'*

He turned and said the patient was not suffering from prostate cancer or any other but an uncommon disease and is dying slowly. A painful death by something called copper-pox-poisoning leaving his private area smelly and decomposing. The doctor said there was no cure for such a sickness and he continued to explain everything in full details."

The reason I am sharing this rare information, is for people who have never heard of it to be educated on the subject.

Superstition in Trinidad and Tobago

This disease is part of the culture of superstition in Trinidad and Tobago and the surrounding Caribbean.

It is considered ***ritual or witchcraft.***

According to the theory or theories here are some of the events that focuses on superstition, that I know to be true in times past but can still exist today.

• There was a traditional way of knowing whether a mother would fully approve of a particular gentleman to wed her daughter by performing 'simidi-mee's' (prayers, chants and rituals) on his personal things and his name.

• Then we have 'stay home sweet rice' which was a way to keep a man from leaving a woman. Before serving him his lunch she would put the plate on the ground first, she would then stoop over the hot food without underwear, allowing the sweat from her vagina to fall in the steaming food. It was believed that as he ate, he would remain 'dotish' (submissive) to her only.

• Parents used to bring home 'baptice people,' (healers who worked in strange magic and were sometimes but not always associated with the Spiritual Baptist religion) with coconut broom, locking you in a room and beating the hell out of you if they thought you were possessed by a spirit. 'Is only bawl you bawling, not because you possessed, but from the pain of the blows you are getting, leaving black and blue marks on your skin.' All of this was done in the hope that the spirit would jump out of your body or else 'is more blows, until you sick, trembling with fear.' Running was not an option because they were in a circle chanting, ringing bells and 'catching off powers,' (jumping to the rhythm of the chant or drum, in a hallucinating shaking state.) Young children would be accused of having a spirit, if they were disobedient or behaved contrary to the rules of the house; if they were sick for too long, sleep-walked, or were mentally ill. These were common reasons for a spiritual intervention or beating.

• People used garlic, salts and pepper and would tie it together with coins in small bags, this would be kept on their body or nearby, to keep away Soucouyants (a night witch that breaks into your house and sucked your blood) from sucking you at night.

• Grannies would wear bingo-bags (very large panties) on the wrong side as a protection from the evil of the night.

• After school mothers would warn their children not to pass through the cemetery when they were coming home, because it was believed that the spirit of the dead will likely follow them into the house.

• People would keep coins under mats, making small bags with powder and coins, placing then in pillows, stitching them in tightly to keep bad spirits away while they slept.

• Just after work, as soon as you reached home, before entering the door you must walk backward, throwing coins over your shoulders as a pre-caution, it was believed that this would keep jumbees (malign spirits) away. If you went to a funeral you would discard your clothes at the door and wash them immediately to keep the spirits of the dead away from your house. Many people would strip at the front door and enter their house in their under-wear after a funeral.

• Then we have the modern-day suspicion where parents would put gold bangles around a baby's wrist and jumbee beads (black bead) around their necks to keep them from getting maljo (a curse of jealousy intent to cause harm) or blight. It is believed that bad luck comes when people were watching or touching them too much.

• Another known belief is 'old wives fables', or tales which is taken as truth but is spurious or superstition. It can be said sometimes to be a type of urban legend, being passed down by an older woman to a younger generation. Such tales are considered superstition, folklore or unverified claims with exaggerated and/or inaccurate details. For example, if you allow someone to sweep your foot, you wouldn't get married; you shouldn't throw away your old hair because someone can use it to put a spell on you; do not pick fruits or leaves of plants at night because something bad may happen to you.

• Coins were also thrown into fountains for well wishes or good luck charms, hoping your dreams will come through. Many cultural superstitions and practices around the world use coins. Coins of every type and kind are celebrated differently.

Many of these superstitions were considered truth and all of these and more used to determine your future or outcome long ago.

1 Timothy 4:7
But refuse profane and old wives' fables, and exercise thyself rather unto godliness.

The Story of Mr. and Mistress Ben

"Remembering the old days between 1970 to 1980's or so, it was a hard rainy season and my parents were in search of a place to live. They needed a spot to build a house, nothing fancy, we just needed a roof over our heads.

So we walked through the bushes in desperation trying to find a piece of land to claim or bargain for. You see, we had been evicted and the four of us were now homeless, we needed somewhere to stay but we couldn't pay rent. With all the stress and frustration on my parents to provide, I felt like my mother and father was ready to give up.

Then we met him, this total stranger, I remembered his voice saying, wait I can help you.

He told us not to worry and to fol-low him, so we went along with this man, through more bushes until finally we found a

place to build, he noted that it was his land and we could build there. He then introduced himself as Mr. Ben. He was tall, dark and strapid (strong and sturdy) with a bald head, big eyes and broad nose. His lips were thick and he had a commanding deep voice.

He asked my parents if they had material to start building and they whispered that they didn't. He noted that he knew of some neighbors around the area who had used galvanize and wood, and may be willing to help. To our surprise, everyone came together and knocked-up a big room, in less than three days, there was one bedroom and one kitchen area. We owned very little furniture, we had a bed and a rolled-up sponge, with a wooden table and two chairs. That was all, we started from scratch but we were together and we had a roof over our heads. We thanked everyone for their help especially Mr. Ben for building us a home.

Soon after they left the rains came, banging down on us, thunder so loud it shook our dwelling and lighting flashed in the dark bush. We placed pots and pans on the floor, the roof was a strainer as the rain poured through the holes towards us. That night we had a lone lantern shining in the darkness, we sat around it and looked at each other all night. There wasn't space to sleep, everything was soaked, even us. By morning when the rain finally stopped, Ben appeared again.

When he saw what happened, he noted he would fix it. He brought a ladder, climbed up to the roof and covered each hole with flash-band. We were again thankful. Afterwards he invited us over to his house for lunch, he didn't live far, we were actually his new neighbors. He introduced us to his common law wife Ma-Ben. She was short and stocky, with a big bottom and she was pretty, a

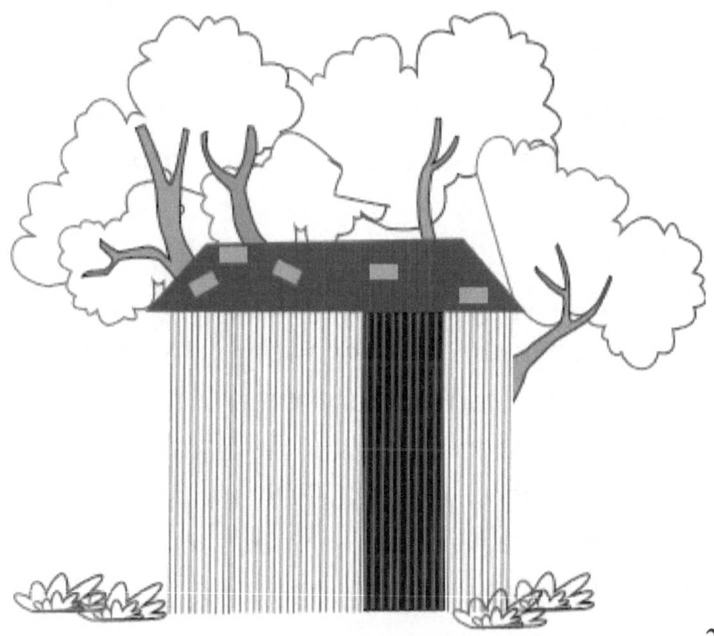

nice brown skin lady who smiled and showed us where we should sit and eat. After lunch Ben gave us a tour of his house, there were two nice bedrooms, one was a guest room, we had already seen the dining room and he showed us the kitchen and a porch area.

He noted that both he and his wife had children but from separate relationships. The house was well furnished, 'put-away' properly, tidy and clean. The man had it nice. Ma-Ben noted they didn't associate too much with neighbors because people were 'maccos' (nosey) and she and her husband had lived here for many years before the others came and built in the neighbourhood. She noted that she was a Tobagoian and she met her husband on a beach in Tobago where they fell in love, which was why she came to Trinidad to live.

She noted that she left her entire family behind. We had a lengthy conversation for hours into the late evening, by then we got to know about each other. While we continued to speak Mr. Ben asked our parents a favor, he asked if my sister and I could look after Ma-Ben and keep her company while he went to work. My parents thought the idea was good, so they agreed.

Mr. Ben, our new neighbor and now good friend was better known as Dude's man, he loved music, he played sparrow and Kitchener on his stereo day and night.

Old stereogram

The following day, as soon as Ben left that morning, my sister and I made preparation in Ma-Ben's kitchen, handling all the necessary things for cooking like washing and cutting up provision, getting water and helping with anything she needed. Knowing Tobagoian food, ah' talking about fish, coocoo, callaloo, curry crab and coconut dumplings.

Sweet hand for so Ben getting.

Although the pot over the fire, Ma Ben busy gathering clothes to wash and rinse in a sink made from concrete. Then she'd be hanging them to dry depending on the weather conditions, because at the end of the day Ben liked everything 'spick and span' and in an orderly manner.

My sister and I enjoyed every moment we spent with Ma Ben, until Uncle Ben came home and as the days and months passed, we began to learn more about the couple. Ma Ben tried her utmost best to please him, to us it seemed as though it was a one-sided love though. Even though we were children and things looked fine to us, Ben worked, his wife stayed home and they had a lovely home with nice furniture and food, but still what she did for Ben, the man never showed much interest in her. At least that is what we witnessed when we were in their home.

At that point in time we couldn't tell if Ben had someone else or not, because Ben was a private man. He was good to my family and helped us out a lot. We continued helping with chores, and after helping we would sit around the table ready to eat, waiting for our food to be dished out into plates with dribble coming from our mouths. Man hungry, because cooking done, but she would always wait five minutes more for Ben's arrival before anyone else could eat. She'd put aside his food first as a rule, making sure he had the best on his plate and then we'd eat.

The way she acted, I felt that she was afraid of him, I just couldn't figure it out. You see Ben wasn't really handsome, it must have been his money because Ben was ugly to me. The saying goes, 'beauty is in the eyes of the beholder' well that was Ben and Ma-Ben. Even though she feared his possessive ways, she loved every inch of Ben, you could see it in her eyes. My sister and I used to wonder what she saw in that man when she was so pretty faced, only God alone knew.

I remembered one time the food was cold because he came late, and he was eating and we pointed out that there were ants in his food and Ben kept eating and said, 'ants ain't have no bone.' Ben was a strange man, he was nice to some people and hard on others, you never knew what he would do until he did it.

When he was finished eating, she would be taking off the shoes from his feet on a daily basis, treating him like some king, putting them away in the bedroom. Most days Ben would follow her to the bedroom and pull the door shut, where he laughed this creepy, 'hay, hay, hay' laugh. Then Ma Ben would say 'doh touch meh; boy no; ah say no; leh me go.' Then we'd hear small slaps and she'd run out the room crying. When we asked what happened, she would always say, 'nothing ah good.'

As children we weren't aware of what was going on and maybe our presence was an issue with Ma-Ben, but when I grew older and learned more about Ben, I realized that whether we were present or not, it would not deter him from being ready for bedroom action.

Ma Ben on the other hand was cautious, she would watch the bedroom door carefully at times when he was in there, looking like she wanted to please him. She'd come and check to see if we were still standing on the porch and say, 'allyuh children still here, allyuh ain't gone home yet?'

We really liked their house, so we would say, 'we

thought you was coming back out, but okay see you tomorrow.'

Their relationship at times would appear perfect yet deceiving. To my observation Ma Ben never really smiled, she was always very tense around us when Ben was home. She hardly spoke to us then, all her focus was on Ben, because of this people opted not to deal with the situation but walked away.

That same night around 10:30 pm, it was a Friday, we heard Ma Ben screaming at the top of her voice but no one knew or could say why. It was late so our parents wouldn't allow us to go over, and we were children so truthfully it was not our business.

We couldn't wait until morning to visit her even though it was the weekend, and what we saw was unbelievable. One of her eyes were black and blue, swollen, we proceeded with caution but before we left we still asked why the black and blue eye? She quickly barred her face with a piece of cloth and ignored our question, she changed the topic and said that we were too young to understand big people business, to leave it alone.

'Okay mam, nuff respect and have a good day,' I said.

On my way home, as I walked through the dirt track, two neighbors who were heading in my direction, on reaching me asked, if me and Ben was good? I said yes, for now but wanted to know why it mattered. They told me things were going good with Ben and his wife over the years and they couldn't understand why recently he started beating his wife so. They noted that he abused Ma Ben regularly and she usually scream for a certain time and then became silent.

Now this was a mystery to me, having found that out, I was even more curious as to what was going on. You see Ben helped my family and we were loyal to him, but I still wanted to find out what was going on with him and Ma Ben. I sincerely felt compelled to go further into the situation and interrogate Ma Ben. I couldn't wait until Monday morning when Ben left for work. When Monday finally came I went over early.

'Good morning mam, how are you?' I greeted her.

'Fine thank you,' she noted.

I knew that she wasn't fine, so I took the opportunity to speak with her because I felt she needed help, I was willing to help her if she asked for help.

That morning Ma Ben was more agreeable and willing to speak and I pushed for her to continue where we left off on Saturday. She admitted that on that day. Mr. Ben was in the back room and she didn't want him to hear anything. She felt embarrassed to share personal information about herself and her relationship with us but knew we had to be curious.

'Yes mam, we know it's personal but how will you receive help by staying silent,' I probed.

She was a bit hesitant at first, but eventually she agreed and told us to keep it among ourselves, because she didn't want Ben to know.

She went on to say that a few years ago had been the darkest moments in her life and people didn't have any idea about Ben and herself, as there wasn't anyone trustworthy enough to confide in. Having these issues made her stressed out and bitter. She stated that as soon as Ben's belly was full all he was interested in was going to the bedroom. Others could go places with their friends or even by themself, but she was just locked down and monitored. He was strategic and us being there to help meant that she was no longer alone, when he wasn't at home. She noted that she was only allowed to go to the grocery on Saturdays and the market on Sundays now, with my sister, who was twelve and her ready 'going-out' companion.

I knew it wasn't my business but I noted that although I was young and I may have even been 'fass' to ask the question, but I wanted to know - Do you sleep together?

Her answer was mixed, she got flustered and said no, then admitted that they used to, and then sometimes they do.

'Why is that?' I probed.

She went on to say that when she said no, he used to beat her a lot until she became so afraid of him that she was peeing herself and not eating because of fear. Now, I was sure it wasn't the food because her hand was tasty.

'Mam, I know I'm a teenager but if you two, as you said, not sleeping in the same bed, then this not adding up,' I decided.

I continued asking questions because I wondered what happened when she said no to him, was that when the harassment from her husband began and did she eventually give in. I wanted to understand what she meant.

Long after, she admitted that the problem was sex, when she wasn't giving him any, he would quarrel plenty and then beat her mercilessly. It took him a while but eventually he just stopped then started back. I felt she should just work out the situation with her husband, as a teenager I was surprised that she and her husband were arguing about sex. They were married and it seemed a simple fix. She noted that there was nothing to work out, and she wasn't wrong, she was tired of Ben.

To our surprise she admitted that when people heard her screaming, it wasn't just the beatings but something he liked to do before he had sex, he would corner her and rip off her clothes, treating her like a stranger. He wanted her to feel like a rape victim and he had different 'kinky' ideas for sex that she didn't like. He was being sexually abusive and would take her multiple times without her consent until he felt good and only then would he fall asleep and leave her alone. She said it was always like that but now she was rebelling, she screamed and confronted him but he did not always leave her alone.

Back then domestic violence was something you worked out on your own, many women suffered at the hands of their husbands and never reported it. Neighbors would hear a woman screaming and just wait until morning to ask what happened. There was no going to the police station, a woman would just return to her family, if she could and that was that.

Ma Ben noted that she had enough and would sleep in the guest room and lock the doors because she was not able with Ben and those things again.

'Ah too old for that,' she said.

'What do you mean?' I wondered out loud.

Ma Ben laughed with her head bent on her lap blushing, and said Ben was something else, that he spelt trouble.

We didn't do anything and Ma Ben endured, she wasn't willing to leave Ben and we were asked not to speak of what she told us.

In life there are coincidences we may encounter, but the words of God shall forever stand firm as said in: Luke 12: 2-3 – 'Nothing is covered up that will not be revealed, or hidden that will not be known. Therefore, whatever you have said in the dark shall be heard in the light, and what you have whispered in private rooms shall be proclaimed on the housetops.'

You see, the following year Ben retired from his government job and somehow he was still on the move every day. We felt that maybe he was working privately and he kept it to himself. Ma Ben told us that she noticed all the tools from his storeroom had gone missing, and it was only him who would have moved them out. She knew that he did private gardening jobs, but he never shared his work life with her.

There was a private primary secondary school around the area and we attended, at Calvary Hill. Parents paid tuition for pupils each term for a period of five years and we were enrolled and settled in. At first we felt strange around new students, learning to get used to going to the school, with new teachers and surroundings.

When you think about it, life is full of surprises, within a year of attending, who could we meet? No one other than Mr. Ben with brooms, a rake and a shovel, a cutlass and other tools pushing his wheelbarrow working as a janitor/caretaker, on said compound.

We were thrilled and rushed forward.

'Hi neighbor, are you working here now?'

His response was yes, he explained that because he was retired, he needed something to occupy himself, and the principal knew his cousin and asked his cousin to recommend a good man to keep the grounds. So his cousin contacted him - mind you Ben didn't have a phone, so if you wanted Ben you had to find him or send a message with someone - and asked if he wanted the job to look after the property. Well we glad for so, seems as though it was the same position he held before he retired.

He told us that from Monday to Friday he stayed at the school and would return home on weekends. We asked him why he didn't work from 8:00 am - 4:00 pm as usual and come home, but he noted that he was also the night watchman during the week, and he had to make sure things were secured. Ben was uneducated, he couldn't read or write but he was a good worker so he advanced in life.

He asked us to continue to check on Ma Ben for him and we agreed but he pleaded with us not to tell Ma Ben about his whereabouts, all she knew was that he was working during the week, but not where he was working. He felt that she fully understood that a man needed to work in order for bills to be paid, that she was just a housewife.

We weren't sure but he noted that furthermore they didn't sleep together anymore, and this was not a new development. We didn't say anything when he noted that a man had needs to fulfill. He argued that he was living with a woman and giving her everything, that he worked hard all his life to build that house and furnish it for them, for her, and paid all the bills.

He said that when a man reached home he wanted to eat his belly full and look for some loving and it didn't make sense, he didn't even get a hug. Ma Ben had changed, she didn't want him to touch her anymore and kept saying that she was fed up and it was only one thing he had on his mind, sex. He felt she was being unfair in their relationship so it was better that he came home on weekends only. We didn't disagree, knowing that they both didn't get along anymore, it seemed best.

The school was situated on a very large compound, which included a private wooden house separated by fencing wire with a gate for the entrance. Looking at the house, it seemed abandoned and certain parts of the yard had plenty bush and vines hanging around. It looked like no one lived there for a while and Ben had lots of work on his hands to get it fixed right. We asked him if he wanted help, but he said he would manage. Watching Ben there I think he was happy, and before leaving him he invited us for dinner the coming Friday and he reminded me to keep an eye on home and I agreed.

When we reached home the first word from our mouth was, 'mammy and daddy we see Mr. Ben in school. They were surprised and wanted to know what he was doing there. We explained that he got a job as the caretaker for the premises and he would be coming home on weekends only. My parents were happy but they wondered who would be staying with Ma Ben in their big house.

We didn't know why Ma Ben couldn't stay by herself, but as her closest neighbor my parents offered for my sister to stay over with Ma Ben at nights. Bright and early the next morning my sister returned saying she hardly slept because Ma Ben talked almost all night about Ben and his nasty habits, which of course she relayed to us.

Even though things were not good between them, Ma Ben professed that she still loved Ben very much and she was missing him as well. She even admitted that she wouldn't mind enduring the music he loudly played every Saturday that she hated. She told my sister that 'woman to woman' every now and again she slept with Ben willingly, when she felt like it but she didn't allow him every day because he got addicted. When she allowed it every day, it was every day after work he would tackle her, all night he would want to be doing this thing, he was never tired. Even when she slept he would wake her up, having sex with her as if he was obsessed or 'some kind of' pervert. She noted that when she finally took control of her body that in addition to the beatings, he would slam doors, break things, and threw tantrums.

She insisted that he never behaved like that for food, if he was hungry but coming to sex, he didn't care to eat, he was crazy, especially if he saw her naked. She was tired and told my sister that

Ben would never get another woman who could cook, clean and wash and put up with him. She was convinced that Ben would not be able to get another woman except her.

So my brother, the next-door neighbor and I made plans to visit Ben on Friday evening. Upon arrival we saw a woman of Indian descent standing next to Ben, she was a tall, slim, shapely, brown skinned in complexion, nice looking lady but she looked younger than Ben. She couldn't be forty yet and Ben was retired, she was much younger than Ma Ben.

Soon, he introduced all of us to his new girlfriend and we stood there in shock and Ben was serious and normal. We never saw it coming; he was excited, full of joy but in my mind I am thinking 'damn foolish man,' ah now see why he want privacy, only eating outside food, that's the reason Ma Ben food not tasting good again and of no interest.'

Soon after the introduction Mr. Ben bent over and whispers in my ear, 'if you know how ah love Indian women, ah just love them."

I couldn't believe it, from my point of view just watching them, I already know this new girl would be Ben's ultimate sex machine, for his pleasure and nothing else. I couldn't believe Ben found someone else so quickly. When everyone gathered around the table to have dinner, what we saw was more like lunch dishes - lots of finger food, all kinds of dishes and drinks (alcohol and non-alcohol). We didn't say a word of prayer, we just start to eat.

Now during dinner we didn't know what was going on as Ben's girlfriend leaves her chair and

went to the bedroom, just a few minutes after Ben followed her, leaving the three of us on the table with all the food without any excuse. It didn't occur to us what was happening, so man continue to eat and drink, watching TV in black and white those days, the three of us enjoyed every minute of it.

Ben and his girlfriend came out of the room half an hour later; she fixing her hair and adjusting her skirt, and Ben smiling, we still didn't put two and two together that night. We just went along with the game, we had fun and that was all we cared about. Ben made things clear that night that we could come every Friday.

"So fellas what you think?"

We agreed wholeheartedly and went home to our respective places and of course it was my duty to check on Ma Ben and not to say a word to her of what I knew.

How time fly, as the day came to return another Friday evening by Mr. Ben, my brother and I remained in our uniform and at school and waited for our friend to meet us on the school compound instead of going home to change and come back. So we showed up early, man hungry, belly in hand, stomach bubbling because we didn't go home and eat, thinking the woman cook and done prepare for her guests, it was not even in the making. No pot on the stove, his kitchen empty, no groceries.

When I turn and look outside the woman was bringing bags towards his wooden house so we cleared the table to make space. It's then I get to know Ben can't cook much less boil an egg and she usually cooked at home and bring the food over to him. Everyone came around and sat, ready to eat then a thought came: 'why this woman and not Ma Ben, for me Ma Ben food taste much better, I was still missing part of the puzzle.'

We kept on visiting Ben, it's all new, being young, knowing very little about man horning (being unfaithful) to their woman and sleeping with other people. We took it as a normal thing. We took note of every visit, and made good observations, for months, they did their routine, the TV was switched on at news time and just after news we watched 'The Incredible Hulk.'

Mr. Ben's girlfriend would leave and go into the

bedroom, where she would not come back to eat; within the next ten minutes Mr. Ben would also leave us and enter the same room. Just before he used to say, 'allyuh please excuse meh, doh worry, eat everything, drink out what you can on the table. Help yourself, okay.'

Then he disappeared inside the room, we never heard a sound from them, because Ben used to max the TV volume, it was so loud that when we tried to speak amongst ourselves we had to come closer just to hear each other speak, it was like a cinema but as children do we soon got bored.

On occasion while Ben together with his woman in the bedroom, we took the bunch of keys for the entire school that he left hanging on a nail in his living room and went exploring. We opened the cafeteria, drinking out juices and eating snacks, once I take a pack of dinner mints to share the next day in school with friends, then children asked.

'Where we get that?'
I told them I bought it in a shop.
'You sure?' someone ask, and I said yes. Sure
enough, someone say I was lying and is thief I
thief it.
'But how allyuh could say them things?' I asked
Because the cafeteria had none, and is dey you
get it from.
'Your mother does only give you five dollars to
come to school,' someone proclaimed.

Man I was ashamed and frightened. How the hell they know that? We return the keys the same night.

The second occasion we took the keys from Ben's table was when he and his woman went off into his chambers, this time I open the form five hall carrying a ladder with me and putting it against a wall, I climbed up and removed about sixteen 6-inch PA speakers from the monitor boxes. We placed the keys where we found it right after.

What happened with the speakers?

They were hooked up on my car deck and equalizer in my mother's house, (I didn't have a car) just blasting music for a couple of days. The principal announced a meeting and the students were told to gather at the Form Five building which held a capacity of four to five hundred persons including my good self. He had papers in hand with mike in the other, the principal tried speaking, testing 1 2 3, again and again. He even tapped the mike but no one heard a sound. Students next to me said the system must be broken or the speakers not working, other students asked what do you think? Well, I don't know. I was sitting with guilt watching the poor man struggle to speak without a mike system.

On the third occasion, it was the same routine with the keys as Mr. Ben and his woman remain in the bedroom to have private conference. Once more I opened the cafeteria but after looking around, for five minutes, suddenly my conscience started to beat me, as to if this was right so I walked back and returned the keys.

Monday morning, as I walked towards the schools' big gate, to my surprise I saw the whole of San Juan police on the compound. They were searching everywhere; I ran and asked a class-mate what happened?

'Boy like bandit broke into the cafeteria but no drinks and snacks missing. The men make a hole in the ceiling stealing all the trophies and medals from the principal's office worth some twenty thousand dollars.'

When I heard that I went back home trembling, running fast to get away from the scene, the things we would do for fun back then could have gotten us into real trouble. Imagine I felt Mr. Ben was horning Ma Ben and we were busy stealing; it was two wrongs that could never make a right.
One night we were just roaming the school yard, minding our own business we hadn't taken the keys again, we were not expecting anyone else to be there and we heard noises.

We couldn't tell exactly where it was coming from so we followed the sound right to the girl's restroom and behold, a man with a 'rasta hair style' just casually walks out the door with a big smile and went his way normal, normal.

A few seconds after a nice 'dougla' (Indian and African mixed) girl comes out of the same door with her school uniform on, and her hair in a mess.

'What the hell?' we thought because she just ignored us.

She passed us quickly and headed for Ben's wooden two room bedroom house, where she skillfully opened a window and climb through it and closed it behind her.

We were shocked.

'What next?" I wondered, and who was this girl and what she doing in there with Ben?

Long after, Ben came out and explained the situation, he noted that the girl was his stepdaughter (his girl-friend child) and she was there to spend the weekend.

It was a whole lot of madness going on with Ben, and none of it made sense, especially to me. I told the fellas I wasn't able with that situation anymore and we should just leave and go home and not return. They didn't agree, they wanted to get to the heart of what was going on with Ben.

"How will we know about Ben, we must finish what we start," they noted.

I agreed, my mind went to Ben and his situation all through the coming days, I wanted to figure out what was going on with Ben so I sat and thought about it. Why would Ben make us come every Friday as a rule? What was the reason? It was suspicious, he recently met his girlfriend and he should have wanted privacy, we may have never known he was being unfaithful to Ma Ben if he hadn't invited us to his new home. Maybe she didn't trust him so he was using us as guests so she could feel welcome and comfortable with him. I didn't believe she had any love for Ben, it looked like games playing. I told myself who in their right mind would lay down under Ben when I remembered what Ma Ben said about him.

During all this commotion we still visiting Ben on Friday, eating his food, roaming the school yard and had learned his routine expertly. He and his new girlfriend would wait until 8pm after the news when the Incredible Hulk started in black and white on TV.

Those days was tube TV's, brands like Curtis Mathes and Sylvania, a 25-inch tabletop or floor model was the most popular. Ben had a Sylvania and each time he switched it on, before it came on you would hear a high pitch, ringing frequency first, then the picture became visible as the tube warmed up.

Ben felt he was bright, telling himself we were young and foolish, but because we were up to no good at first, he felt we didn't care. I imagined then that Ben was horning Ma Ben, right in our presence and we were busy with those keys opening and closing every door in the school, getting kicks, doing mischief and never paying attention to why both of them leaving us around the table with food and drinks and the volume on max, watching Bill Bixby turn into a green Lou Ferrigno. But the more I thought about it, the more I needed to know for sure so I plan for Ben. I wanted to know why he and his girlfriend always disappearing inside the bedroom.

First I learned always to be aware of your sur-roundings, have some speculation and be opti-mistic, then investigate and work according to suit. One day when Ben was working around the school compound, I watched him as he swept the yard then picked up the leaves from the ground and placed it in his wheelbarrow. I also noticed that Ben took up all the coins from the ground that fell from the students and placed them in his pocket. I kept track of him as he worked, my eyes following his movements until he was working around the corner. Then, I snuck around the back of his plywood house, where the bedroom was, with a Phillips screwdriver and one large gypsum screw, which was used to bore three holes, in order to see some action in that bedroom.

We even tested our eyes peeping through the holes, we were determined to get a clear view. I needed to find out if he was having an affair on Ma Ben for sure, because that was the only explanation from walking away from good food and drink

Inside Ben's room there was one bed, a chest of drawers with a mirror and a medium sized wardrobe. As we continued taking turns testing our eyes my brother saw a wooden ledge with a heap of coins at the corner of the room. Being caught up in situations is not easy, especially when its nosy school children in big people business.

We waited anxiously. Soon Friday came, the three of us alongside Ben and his girl sat at the table asking God to bless the meal before dining. As we ate both their eyes were on each other, having no appetite for food, they ate very little then got up and excused themselves to the bedroom.

Ah ha! With no time to waste, I surmised that it was 'action time fellas!'

We snuck to the back of the house and positioned ourselves each man to a peep hole, every man to order. My brother whispered that he was only seeing the middle portion, my neighbor was only seeing the head area. At my position, I snickered because from my spot I was seeing their entire body.

Who say I didn't see? I see.

Ben got caught in the act, both of them naked as they born.

Oh my goodness! I am telling you when I see Ben and his exposure, I was shocked.

You could swear he was 'Mandingo' because there was no 'donkey-toe' bigger than Mr. Ben's asset, no wonder Ma Ben refused him and would rather take licks to escape what was in his pants.

I felt that by law it would have been a criminal act of misconduct against her constitutional rights. We were stunned as we watched Ben through that peep hole and we couldn't peal our eyes away.

His girlfriend said, 'Honey come nah, I want to get over with it."

Looking at Ben, how in the world she could get over it, or under it, the possibility out of 100% was about 20% take. I could not believe this woman, she had to be wicked to herself, she probably got used to it, or was just making up her mind before disaster strike. Ben walked over, saying okay love and stopped, when she asked him what happened? He said you know how them dogs does stand on four legs oh like so; you want it doggie style. She agreed and turned and he positioned her how he wanted her. By then, we were watching in awe, our young minds were blown.

To me she was not pleased doing any of that, just the expression on her face when she turned away from him said it all. Her face was horrified, as Ben laughed hay, hay, hay and said, 'Girl if you know how ah love ah Indian woman, ah does get weak.'

He grabbed on to her in desperation doing the 'boogaloo.'

Ben's face happy, he feeling sweet, but her face scrounge up and soon she begged him to hurry up because it was hurting.

'Ben stop, you hurting me.'

He listened to her and said 'I go done just now.'

Ben reached climax, shouting out how much he loved the woman, and cried out for God over and over. When it was over, he was smiling happily asking her if she was alright, professing still that she was sweet for so, but she looked like she was in pain. She was bleeding, he cleaned her up with tissue paper, but that poor woman looked like she was suffering from a womb problem or was on her monthly cycle.

While she sat on the bed, Ben walked over to where his pants were hanging and retrieved some money from the pocket and placed it in her hand and said thank you. Ben like he was paying for sex, which was why she came every Friday because that was when Ben got paid.

I understood his relationship now but it still didn't explain why he kept inviting us.

This was a once in a lifetime adventure, being there to see and hear everything, we finally pried our eyes away and ran into the school yard laughing, we rolled on the grass, tears streaming down our face because we couldn't laugh as hard as we wanted for fear that Ben would figure out what we were up too.

We remained playing in the courtyard under false pretenses, until they passed us smiling and saying goodnight as he walked her home.

Mr. Ben was a clean and tidy man who always inspected his surroundings, he often swept the yard twice per day, cutting the lawn grass before it grew too high. So before there was any suspicion with three holes in the wall of his house, I took some grass with moss and placed them over the holes before we left, to cover up the evidence of our dirty works.

The following Monday after school was dismissed, I passed by Ben still in my school uniform, he was trimming the overgrown vines on the fence to the back of his house, he was staring and pointing at the pieces of grass on the plywood questioning how it got there. Luckily he blamed the birds and walked away.

Our mission was accomplished, that night with all the evidence pointed at him, that he was cheating the entire time, and by the looks of it, it was no romantic relationship but more like a paid private escort, and using us as scapegoats (alibi) so people wouldn't suspect he was doing anything while we were there. We agreed that there was no reason to go back there every Friday, and keep getting in between him and Ma Ben business. Ma Ben was still our dear neighbor and friend and Ben hadn't admitted to her that he moved on.

Ben used to give us money to drop for Ma Ben but it became infrequent. Suddenly he had no money to send because the next woman eating him out. Ma Ben's family used to send her food and money with people when they came down on the boat from Tobago in that way she didn't starve. Back then women who were housewives like Ma Ben didn't work and we felt sorry that Ben left her and blamed him, because she never worked, and always depended on him.

She noted that she wanted to leave and go back to Tobago but she stayed and waited for Ben to return. Ben on the other hand had moved on, he picked up a new woman and Ben wasn't a young boy, he was retired in his early sixties while Ma Ben was in her early fifties. It was clear that if Ma Ben was not willing to give him sex, then he felt they had no relationship, but he hadn't admitted to her that he had another woman.

Mind you he still went home to Ma Ben on week-ends, just to check on his house maybe but he didn't stay long. By then Ma Ben knew where he worked and stayed during the week but I got so upset seeing Ma Ben in need, that I never stepped foot on his path again, we just went from home to school and back, and kept an eye on Ma Ben.

Now that we were staying away, I noticed at one time that the school compound hadn't been cleaning as usual. For three weeks it looked unkept and I began to wonder what was going on. One day the principal explained that the groundskeeper Mr. Ben was not feeling well, which was why we had unkept surroundings but she didn't want to bring strangers to do the job.

So the teachers asked if we would cooperate and help clean, we didn't hesitate we got his brooms, rake, shovel and wheelbarrow and cleaned the yard and walkway as best as we could.

Now that I knew that Ben was sick, I passed by Ma Ben on my way home and told her what happened at school. She asked me what he was sick with, but I couldn't say. I decided then that I was going to pay him a visit and find out more. Ma Ben admitted that he hadn't come home for three weeks, so the illness explained his absence. When she asked me when the last time was that I saw him, I admitted that we hadn't visited him for a while and got the news from the principal, not him.

She asked if me and Ben fell out but I said no, he was just busy and I was busy with school. We attempted to persuade Ma Ben to go and see Ben, but she insisted that she was not going, she said: 'I never send him there and he keepin' secrets from me so let whoever it is taking care of him, take care of him.'

I couldn't say anything because it seemed as if she guessed or knew what was going on with Ben and the woman.

The next day I left for school, when I arrived my attention was on Ben, even though he treated Ma Ben badly, I went and checked on him. On entering his front door there was a Chinese man, dressed in a white coat and black pants with his medical kit who I assumed was the doctor.

I said good day and went straight to Ben, his girlfriend at his bedside. She wept inconsolably, holding on to him, he noted that he was going to a better place and that he loved her and she continued to hug Ben.

Then I said to Ben, God knows best we are praying for you, with one hand stretch out holding the end of my school shirt, Ben said: 'Tell Ma Ben I sorry for putting her through problems and to forgive me.'

I agreed and his girlfriend watch both of us and ask Ben how it is that she now hearing about another woman, Ben told her not to worry it was a long story love. She didn't probe further because he said it was too late for that now.

In the meanwhile, I spoke to the doctor to one side asking what was the real problem with Mr. Ben? He went on to say that Ben complained of excruciating pain about his belly and groin area and each time he urinated the colour changed. He had no appetite and was looking pale, with a rash on his stomach and between his legs.

The doctor said that his checks and blood test results confirmed that what he had was very serious. I was present, a witness when he revealed the shocking news that this most likely was done by a woman with whom he slept with. Then I saw his girlfriend gazing in our direction, as she tried to hear the conversation. The doctor asked her to excuse him with Ben for a few minutes, because he needed to chat with him, Ben noted that I could stay.

Ben asked how and what sickness is this?

The doctor noted that it was an uncommon disease that can only be passed from a woman to a

man during sex, where the woman places a five-cent piece in her mouth under the tongue unknowingly to the man, sucking on it until enough copper is built up in her saliva waiting for the man to ejaculate. The copper now has free entry into the man's blood stream through his private part. Ben listened attentively and began to cry, he admitted that he had only slept with three women, his children's mother, Ma Ben and his girlfriend.

He and his children's mother separated years ago, Ma Ben was his common law wife (they were not married but lived together long enough for a union to be acceptable by law) and now his current lover, and she was the last person he slept with.

'So doc who really do this to me?' he asked

The doctor noted it was a private matter and he couldn't involve himself in that part of the situation. Mr. Ben begged and pleaded for the doctor to heal him, promising to pay any amount, he said the pain was as if someone was holding his groin and squeezing them.

The doctor could not, he noted only God could help Ben but he was willing to give him two injections per day to help with the pain. He said it would help Ben to sleep but otherwise he was sorry because he believed that Ben didn't have much time to live, there was no cure and his privates were already decomposing. His only advise was that Ben make peace with God.

We stood with Ben in prayer and he asked God to forgive all his wrongs. He said, Lord please forgive me of all my sins that I have done and for the people and the animals I have hurt. Thank you Lord Amen.

I returned and stayed a while with Ben before going home that day.

However that said night, Ben better known as Uncle Ben, aka Dudes man, passed away peacefully at the wooden house located at Calvary Hill, San Juan. Cause of death was listed as Copper Pox poisoning.

Days after his death during school hours we saw a white pick-up van parked outside the gate with Ben's girlfriend and two other men removing all the furniture and appliances leaving the tiny two-bedroom house empty and abandoned as before.

*****

As I grew older my mind would think about Ben, he saved my family from homelessness and for that we were forever grateful. I didn't understand his ways when I was a youth, it was either him or Ma Ben and he was a cruel man at times, especially to animals.

It was only when I grew older and encountered the dynamics of relationships did the situation begin to make sense. I still didn't agree with his treatment of

Ma Ben, I felt he should have just broken it off and let her return to her family but Ben was a possessive man.

He didn't deserve to die like that, and I often queried about this disease and how it was inflicted, it became an obsession with me to find out more about it and to understand it. I can't say that I have done so, but in documenting this story I have released it and Ben.

- The End

Types of Pox

Taken from Wikipedia online

1. Chickenpox, a highly contagious illness caused by a primary infection with varicella zoster virus (VZV)
2. Plum pox, the most devastating viral disease of stone fruit from the genus "Prunus"
3. Canarypox, a disease of wild and captive birds
4. Cowpox, a rodent disease that can infect cattle, and also transmissible to humans
5. Fowlpox, an infectious disease of poultry
6. Goatpox, an infectious disease of goats
7. Horse pox, an infectious disease of horses
8. Monkeypox, an infectious rodent disease that can infect primates
9. Mousepox, an iatrogenic infectious disease of laboratory mice
10. Rabbitpox, an iatrogenic infectious disease of laboratory rabbits
11. Pigeon pox, an infectious disease of pigeons
12. Sheeppox, an infectious disease of sheep
13. Smallpox, an eradicated infectious disease unique to humans, caused by either of two virus variants – bleeding under the skin
14. Squirrel pox, an infectious disease of squirrel
15. Swinepox, an infectious disease of swine
16. Rickettsialpox, a rickettsial disease spread by mites.
17. Syphilis, also known as grande verole, the "great pox", a sexually transmitted disease caused by the spirochetal bacteria Treponema pallidum
18. White pox disease, a coral disease

Coins of Trinidad and Tobago
https://worldcoinsinfo.com/world/trinidad-tobago-coins.html

Dominion of the Great Britain Trinidad and Tobago (1962-1976)
Trinidad and Tobago Dollar=100 cents

1 dollar 1969
Copper-nickel / commemorative coin
FOOD FOR ALL / 1 DOLLAR
REPUBLIC OF TRINIDAD AND TOBAGO 1969
Coin value - $3-4

50 cents 1966
copper-nickel
TRINIDAD AND TOBAGO
Coin value - $4-6

25 cents 1966
copper-nickel
TRINIDAD AND TOBAGO
Coin value - $1

10 cents 1966
copper-nickel
TRINIDAD AND TOBAGO
Coin value - $1

10 cents 1976
copper-nickel
TRINIDAD AND TOBAGO
Coin value - $1

5 cents 1966
bronze circulation coinage
TRINIDAD AND TOBAGO
Coin value - $1

5 cents 1972
bronze commemorative coin
10th Anniversary of
Independence
TRINIDAD AND TOBAGO
Coin value - $5-7

1 cent 1973
bronze circulation coinage
TRINIDAD AND TOBAGO
Coin value - $1

1 cent 1975
bronze circulation coinage
TRINIDAD AND TOBAGO
Coin value - $1

1 cent 1972
bronze commemorative coin
10th Anniversary of Independence
TRINIDAD AND TOBAGO
Coin value - $3-4

1977 Copper-Nickel Commemorative Coin
ONE DOLLAR
REPUBLIC OF TRINIDAD AND TOBAGO
Coin value - $10-12

1979 Copper-Nickel Commemorative Coin
1 DOLLAR / FOOD FOR ALL
REPUBLIC OF TRINIDAD AND TOBAGO
Coin value - $3-4

1995 Copper-Nickel Commemorative Coin
50th Anniversary of FAO
FOOD FOR ALL / 1 DOLLAR /
FAO 50TH ANNIVERSARY 1945-1995
REPUBLIC OF TRINIDAD AND TOBAGO
Coin value - $2-3

50 cents 2003
copper-nickel
REPUBLIC OF TRINIDAD AND TOBAGO
Coin value - $1

25 cents 2003
copper-nickel
TRINIDAD AND TOBAGO
Coin value - $1

10 cents 2008
copper-nickel
TRINIDAD AND TOBAGO
Coin value - <$1

5 cents 2009
bronze
TRINIDAD AND TOBAGO
Coin value - $1

1 cent 2010
bronze
TRINIDAD AND TOBAGO
Coin value - $1

About the Author

Mr. Karcian Suragh

I am a proud Trinidadian man born in the year 1966. I am a single father of two and I am not ashamed to say that I have no credentials of any kind. For me, I really try my best to be creative and be true with my work whether it is writing a book or working on some type of electronic item.

My first book 'HIV/Aids, is a chance ah go take' was similar, as it spoke to true life experiences and my memory of those I met, who died and lived with the disease. It's not medical or scientific but tells the story of the people and gives a glimpse into their everyday lives. Before making this second book about copper pox poisoning, it took a lot of contemplation over the years, getting my facts and memories together but it is a story I had to tell. So, I hope this book is informative and educational, persons must be observant in their relationships, around friends, associates and even family members.

In everything you do put God first and man after, some of my hobbies are praying to God on mornings, writing, electronics, nature, all kinds of music, cooking a good pot with my children, and a little bad habit at times, drinking socially with friends.

No one knew when they were born and no one remembers falling asleep; a form of death while our bodies lay motionless as the unconscious mind dreams into another zone. Hoping that the mercy of God wakes us. Life is short, live with purpose and be true to yourself and others.

HIV AIDS Why Me?
Is a Chance ah go take!

This book contains real-life stories of the spread of the HIV epidemic. The circle of relationships, mistakes made and the final consequence. While reading I hope and pray that you may learn a lesson from these stories. There are not many words to replace or substitute more than the original ones, fiction I can add but true and real stories such as these must be told as is.

This book clearly shows a wide range of risk and behaviour of persons who took great chances with their lives. Thereafter, you will be able to see that in situations like these no one is perfect or has a shield of covering around them. No one is invincible, it matters not whether you are black, white, Spanish, Indian, Chinese; man or woman; boy or girl; rich or poor, this can happen to any one of us as human beings.